the No Biggie bunch™

Dairy-Free Dino-Licious Dig

For all kids who like to explore,
especially those with dairy
allergies and courage galore!

LIBRARY OF CONGRESS CONTROL NUMBER: 2009910180
ISBN 978-0-9822150-3-6

P.O. Box 95024
Newton, Massachusetts 02495
www.parentperksinc.com

Authors: Heather Mehra and Kerry McManama
Illustrations: ©Michael Kline Illustration (dogfoose.com)
Design: JoeLeeDesign.com

Printed in China
CPSIA Section 103(a) Compliant:
Tracking ID: K0113414
Tracking No: K9411987-6460
www.beaconstar.com/Consumers/

the No Biggie bunch ™

Dairy-Free Dino-Licious Dig

BY

Heather Mehra & Kerry McManama

ILLUSTRATIONS BY

Michael Kline

FOR KIDS CREATIVELY COPING WITH FOOD ALLERGIES

"Dinosaur hunting is my favorite thing to do!"

Davis exclaimed as he and Natalie
ran into her backyard.

Davis was ready to dig. "Natalie, you've got the best backyard! It's so big — big enough to hold a whole dinosaur!" he said.

Davis looked all around, took a few careful steps and said, "Right here! This is the perfect place to start the excavation."

"The dinosaur dig. This is where we're gonna find the scaliest, toothiest, biggest dinosaur ever!" Davis declared.

"C'mon, let's get started."

And dig they did, that unstoppable
No Biggie Bunch duo.

The pint-sized paleontologists shoveled grass, dirt and pebbles. After a while, they paused to check out their handiwork.

"Dinosaur digging makes me hungry," Natalie said. "What do you have in your No Biggie Bag?"

Davis unzipped his No Biggie Bag. His dinosaur book fell out and he found his dairy-free snack. He never went on an adventure without either one.

Urp!

Natalie reached for her No Biggie Bag. She packed some cheese crackers and her Safety Searchlight for the adventure. "I just love cheese crackers! Do you think dinosaurs like them?" she asked.

"Yep, I know they do!" Davis exclaimed, "but I can't share the snack. I'm allergic to the milk in the cheese."

"Bummer!"

Natalie scowled.

"No biggie!"

"I have my own crackers. They don't have any dairy in them. They're safe for me to eat. And, they're dino-licious!"

"I bet dinosaurs like your crackers, too," Natalie added.

"Absolutely!"

Davis said as he revealed a
T-Rex-sized grin. "But I hope
the dinosaurs aren't hungry
today. I'm going to eat them
all up myself!"

Natalie laughed. "Well, there's only one thing left to do..."

"DIG!"

CLINK

Just then Davis's shovel hit something.

"Quick, Natalie," he said, "Grab your
Safety Searchlight. I think I hit a
Pterodactyl bone!"

CITY OF NEWTON
WATER DEPARTMENT

No Biggie Bag Bonus

Which safe snacks and supplies would
you pack for your dinosaur dig?

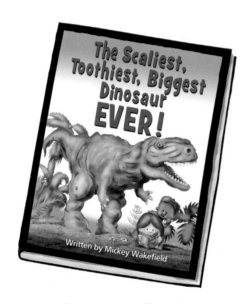

Dinosaur Book

**Dairy-Free
Dino-Licious Crackers**

Safety Searchlight

Greta

Greetings from outer space! I'm Greta. I'm allergic to gluten.

Scotty

Hey, sports fans! My name is Scotty. I'm allergic to Soy.

Paige

I'm Paige, the fairest princess in all the land. I'm allergic to peanuts.

Meet the No Biggie Bunch

Davis

Hello, fellow explorers. I'm Davis and I love dinosaurs. I'm allergic to dairy.

Natalie

Hi, friends. My name is Natalie and I'm artsy. I have no food allergies.

Eliot

Howdy, partners! They call me Cowboy Eliot. I'm allergic to egg.

The Mission of the No Biggie Bunch

The No Biggie Bunch is a diverse group of kids who handle the social challenges of food allergies with poise and panache.

The adventures of Davis, Natalie, Paige, Eliot, Scotty and Greta are neither technical nor medical. Their stories are meant to act as springboards for conversation among children, parents, teachers, friends and family members.

The No Biggie Bunch doesn't speak about limitations or medications. They focus on allergen-free celebrations and smart preparation.

Focus on fun and all you can do and soon you'll be saying,

"No Biggie" too!